The people of Etheria love their Princess Adora, who is gentle and good. But there are times when Princess Adora becomes She-Ra, Princess of Power, riding Swift Wind, her winged unicorn. Those are the times when she has magic powers to defend the country against the forces of evil, or simply to help someone in trouble.

British Library Cataloguing in Publication Data
Grant, John. *1930-*
　　Catra's ice palace.—(She-Ra princess of power.)
　　I. Title　　II. Senior, Geoffrey　　III. Series
　　823'.914[J]　　PZ7
　　ISBN 0-7214-1000-6

First edition

Published by Ladybird Books Ltd　Loughborough　Leicestershire　UK
Ladybird Books Inc　Lewiston　Maine 04240　USA

Catra's Ice Palace

by John Grant
illustrated by Geoff Senior

Ladybird Books

It was mid-winter in Etheria. The snow lay crisp over field and forest. Against the blue sky, the Crystal Castle glittered in the frosty air.

The Etherians enjoyed winter. They laughed and sang as they went into the woods to cut logs for their fires. They built snowmen. They skated on the frozen lakes and rivers. And the younger ones had marvellous snowball fights.

4

The people of Whispering Wood enjoyed their
winter fun as much as anyone. The Twiggets jumped
and rolled in the snow. They made a slide which
even Kowl enjoyed, although he had to admit that
he was hardly built for that sort of thing. After several
tumbles, he went off to his secret store in a hollow
tree. Then, he produced a great bag of chestnuts.
Bow lit a fire, and they all feasted on roast chestnuts
until darkness fell and it was time to go home.

Far from Whispering Wood, on the edge of the Fright Zone, stood a sinister tower: the lair of the wicked Catra and her mischief-making friends.

Unlike the Crystal Castle, Catra's tower did not glitter against the sky. The stone walls were grey and damp, and sprinkled with frost where the north wind blew from the Fright Zone. Grey slush and ice lay among the cracks and crevices of the stones. Jagged icicles hung from the edge of the roof and over the windows.

Inside, only a few rooms were kept warm by fires. The rest of the stairs and passages dripped with water. Freezing draughts blew under the doors.

Catra stood on the highest point of her tower. She shook her fist at the distant Crystal Castle.

"Some day, *I* shall have a Crystal Castle!" she cried. "No! I will have a Crystal *Palace*! When I have shown She-Ra and her creatures who is the real ruler around here!"

While Catra shivered in her gloomy tower, Princess Adora and her friend Glimmer went riding in the snowy countryside. Everything was very beautiful. Green mistletoe shone against the dark trunks of the oak trees. A robin perched on a sprig of holly and whistled to them as they passed. The holly and the ivy made dark patterns against the white of the snow. There was no wind, and the noon-day sun was warm.

Glimmer said, "It's good to be out of doors on a day like this. It's almost warm enough for a picnic."

"What a good idea," said Adora. "But instead of just a picnic, why don't we have a winter carnival? We could hold it by the lake near Castle Brightmoon. The lake is frozen and we could have skating, as well as singing and dancing."

"And eating and drinking," said Glimmer.

"And prizes... for building snowmen, and for races on the ice," said Adora.

"AND," said Glimmer, "we could invite Frosta, the Ice Empress, to be guest of honour. It's usually too warm for her to come to summer parties."

"If we are going to do all that," said Adora, "we'd better get started right away."

The first thing to do was to invite Frosta to be guest of honour. Adora and Glimmer rode back to Castle Brightmoon and wrote the invitation.

Frosta's reply came in a few days. She said that she would be delighted to come.

"Who else should we invite?" said Glimmer.

"There's no need to invite people," said Adora. "Anyone who wants to can come. All our friends and neighbours will want to come... and to help. Everyone can do their bit. And everyone can join in the fun."

"But," said Glimmer, "what about people like Catra and her friends? Do we really want them at our winter carnival?"

"Why not?" said Adora. "For all her wicked ways, I don't think that Catra is a very happy person. If she comes, we must make her welcome."

News of the winter carnival spread quickly.
Everyone was very excited, and they talked about
nothing else.

It was not long before word reached the Fright Zone.

Castaspella brought the news to Catra. "Anyone
can attend," she said. "It might be fun."

Catra thought for several long moments. "So, it's
fun they want," she purred. "I think that they should

have more fun than they bargain for. Here is my chance to repay all the times that my plans have been upset by those interfering busybodies."

"How will you do that?" asked Castaspella.

"I don't know, yet," said Catra. "But I will think of something. And it will be extra-special. I will wait until all their preparations are made. That may give me an idea or two."

Soon everyone was hard at work.

A crowd of Twiggets scurried about on the frozen lake with branches of fir, sweeping the ice clear of snow. Then they marked out, with brightly coloured flags, places for skating races, figure skating contests, and other competitions.

Around the shore of the lake, tents and pavilions and stalls were set up. Seats were set for the spectators, and long tables for the feast which was an important part of the winter carnival.

Away from the lake, others were just as busy.
They cooked and baked the food for the feast.
Madame Razz magicked away like mad producing
sweet cakes. Some even turned out the way she
intended! And Kowl went back to his secret store in
the hollow tree for more chestnuts to be roasted and
eaten on the day.

Last of all, when the Twiggets had finished
clearing the snow from the lake, they went off into
the woods and came back with armfuls of holly and
ivy to decorate everything.

Catra listened to the reports that reached her of the preparations at the lake. It was time to decide what she could do to liven up the proceedings, she thought. She turned to Clawdeen, who was sprawled out in front of a blazing fire. "Now, I will have to see for myself," she said. "Take me to the lake."

Clawdeen opened one eye. "It is cold outside," she growled. "Everything is covered with snow. I do not like snow. It gets in my fur and freezes my pads. Go by yourself." And she stretched herself, yawned loudly and went to sleep.

Catra tried to nudge her awake, but Clawdeen took no notice.

"I'll still find out," said Catra, and she climbed the stairs to the topmost part of her tower. She stepped out on the flat roof to where there was a metal lever. Brushing snow from the lever, Catra pulled, and with a loud creaking, part of the stone swung open. Out of the opening rose a slender metal tube in an intricate metal frame.

"Let's see what the catscope can show me," said Catra, putting her eye to one end of the tube. Then she swung the catscope until she was looking at the distant lake.

The day of the winter carnival came at last. From early in the morning the people began to arrive, carrying baskets of food and bottles of drink.

Musicians unpacked their instruments and took their places in a bandstand which had been set up beside the lake.

The crowds grew. The band played merry airs, and the flags flapped cheerfully in the breeze. Fires had been lit here and there around the lake, and

people warmed themselves and chatted to their friends as they waited.

At last, the trumpeters blew a loud fanfare. There was a clatter of hooves and a jingle of sleigh-bells. Then there came a loud cheer as Frosta, the Ice Empress, swept across the lake driving her silver sleigh pulled by four white ponies.

Adora rode up on Spirit to greet the Ice Empress, and lead her to the seat of honour.

The winter carnival had begun.

As the games grew fast and furious on and around the lake, Catra watched from her tower. Through the powerful lens of the catscope she could see every detail.

She watched the young men as they raced on skates across the ice. And she saw Frosta present the prize to the winner. She was too far away to hear the music, but she saw the figure skaters swoop and glide and pirouette in graceful patterns.

She swung the catscope to one side. A pair of young Twiggets had crept behind a tent where food was being prepared and were helping themselves to a hot pie each. They scurried away when the cook shouted after them. One of them dropped his steaming pie as he ran, and as it hit the snow, the snow melted and the pie sank out of sight.

Catra didn't wait to see any more. She knew what she was going to do. But – she had some work to do first.

It was close to midday when the judging of the snowman competition was announced. The snowmen stood along the edge of the lake, and the competitors hurriedly put last-minute touches to their work as Frosta walked along the line.

They were all splendid. But the one which was most admired, and was certain to win a prize, had been built by the Twiggets. It was a snowman of Kowl! Kowl looked at it. He walked all around it. "Hm!" he said. "Not a bad likeness, although you've made me look fat!"

"But, Kowl," said the oldest Twigget, "you're not

exactly..." Then, he stopped. Something was
happening to the snow Kowl. It was leaning
sideways. The beak fell off. And then the fingers. It
was melting. And so was the snow round about it.

It was noon. The sun was at its highest. But it was
not hot enough to melt the snow. And now other
snowmen began to melt. Everyone backed away.

Adora looked beyond the lake. Far, far away she
saw a dazzling light, coming from the direction of
Catra's tower.

Adora slipped away from the crowd. "This is a
task for She-Ra, Princess of Power!" she said.

Out of sight of the crowd, Adora drew her sword. She held it aloft and cried:

"FOR THE HONOUR OF GRAYSKULL!"

and in a moment she had become Princess She-Ra! Mystic light blazed from the sword upon Spirit, and he was transformed into Swift Wind, the fabulous winged unicorn.

Quickly, She-Ra mounted. "Up, Swift Wind," she cried, and they rose high into the frosty air. She-Ra turned Swift Wind towards the Fright Zone, where the mysterious blaze of light was still shining. Catra was up to her mischief again.

From high above, She-Ra looked down on the tower, and saw Catra bending over a piece of apparatus. It was the catscope – but Catra had re-arranged it. The powerful telescope lens now formed a giant burning glass. Catra was aiming the sun's rays at the distant winter carnival. She had already destroyed the snowmen, and she was playing the rays on the ice of the lake. As it began to melt, people ran in terror for the safety of the bank.

She-Ra turned back and made for the lake. She had an idea.

As Swift Wind touched down on the snow, She-Ra called, "Frosta! Come quickly! I need your help!"

Frosta ran to Swift Wind, carrying her magic sceptre in her hand. Quickly, she leapt up behind She-Ra. Swift Wind's powerful wings carried them high above the lake and across the snowy land towards the Fright Zone.

A safe distance from the tower, Swift Wind hovered in the air. Catra was keeping the burning-glass trained on the lake and didn't notice them.

Frosta raised her sceptre high above her head, and a stream of ice crystals came from the centre. She

wove the sceptre to and fro, and the crystals began
to join together to make a wide glittering disc. The
disc hung in the still air, held by the power of
Frosta's sceptre. Then – the Ice Empress guided the
disc round until it caught the ray from Catra's glass.

Catra jumped back at the dazzle of light which
suddenly appeared. It reflected back on her tower.
Frosta moved it slightly, and the sun was directed on
to the snow-covered roof above Catra's head. Catra
made to jump clear… but she was too late. With a
slither and a thump, the snow slid loose and buried
her up to the neck.

She-Ra aimed with her sword, and a bolt of
energy shattered the lens of the catscope.

Leaving Catra floundering in the snow, She-Ra and Frosta flew back to rejoin the winter carnival.

There was nothing to be done about the melted snowmen, but Frosta quickly used her powers to re-freeze the lake for the skaters.

It was now time for the feast. The tables were piled high with good things, and soon the sounds of happy voices were almost drowned by the rattle of plates and cups and saucers.

At the tower, Catra had dug herself free. "I *must* have my revenge!" she shouted furiously at Clawdeen. "You've *got* to take me to the lake. *Now*!"

"Anything for a quiet life," grumbled Clawdeen. And a few moments later she was galloping across the snow with Catra on her back.

The feast was still going on. Nobody noticed Catra and Clawdeen as they crept up under cover of the tents. Then Catra heard a munching sound. It was Frosta's ponies feeding from nose bags.

They were still harnessed to the sleigh, and with a wicked laugh, Catra leapt into the seat and seized the reins. Just at that moment, the ponies caught the scent of Clawdeen and Catra. With squeals of terror they reared up... then raced, out of control, across the lake.

Frosta jumped up as she heard her ponies squealing.

She-Ra had changed back to Adora. "It's Catra," she cried. "She's stealing your sleigh."

"I don't think so," said Frosta. "But she wanted a ride in my sleigh – so let's give her one!"

From a fine chain around her neck she took a small, silver whistle. She put it to her lips and sent a few sweet notes trilling across the frozen lake. At the sound, the careering ponies slowed to a trot. They pricked up their ears and came towards their

mistress. "Welcome to the feast, Catra!" she cried. "Before you eat, a sleigh ride is just the thing to give you an appetite."

She blew another note on the silver whistle and the ponies leapt forward at a fast gallop. Catra lost her hold on the reins. She clung with both hands to the sides of the sleigh. It was all she could do to prevent herself being thrown out as the ponies twisted and turned at high speed to Frosta's commands.

31

At length, Adora said, "I think Catra's had enough. Stop the sleigh."

Frosta blew her whistle once more. The ponies came to a sudden stop. The sleigh spun sideways and almost tipped over, and as it righted itself, they saw that Catra had been thrown out on the ice. Then the ponies galloped to where Frosta was waiting.

As the sleigh stopped, there came a cry from Catra. "I'm not beaten yet! You were very foolish to leave this pretty thing in your sleigh!"

She was holding something above her head, something which glittered in the winter sunshine.

"Catra has your sceptre!" cried Adora. "It must have been in the sleigh!"

"Yes," said Frosta. "I put it there to be out of the way while I ate. But, don't worry. The sceptre is useless in the hands of someone as wicked as Catra. She might even find it dangerous."

Catra stood in the centre of the lake. She waved the magic sceptre over her head in triumph. And the sceptre began to glow with mystic light. The head became an ever-changing pattern of ice crystals. A strange, icy-blue glow shone from the sceptre, and formed a bubble of light around Catra. She began to feel afraid.

"What's happening?" cried Adora.

"The sceptre is taking its own revenge on one who would steal it," said Frosta.

"Can't you stop it?" asked Adora.

"Any time I choose," said Frosta, with a smile. "But I think that I will leave it alone for the moment. It may teach Catra a lesson on the folly of stealing other people's property."

Catra threw down the sceptre and made to run for the bank of the lake. But she could go no further than the shimmering blue light. It was like a solid wall. She was trapped!

"Clawdeen! Help! Come quickly!" cried Catra.

The big cat bounded from the reeds by the lakeside and raced across the ice towards Catra.

"Get me out of here!" cried Catra.

"What's all the fuss?" growled Clawdeen. "It's only a blue light, not a brick wall!" And she jumped through the blue bubble to Catra's side. "Jump on my back," she growled. "We'll be out of here in two swishes of a tiger's tail."

Next moment, Clawdeen was sitting on the ice with a paw to her head. She had bounced back from the shimmering wall of light. The sceptre had let her in... but not out!

She was trapped along with Catra.

The sceptre was still lying on the ice. "It's all the fault of that stupid thing!" cried Catra. She picked it up and threw it hard. It passed unharmed out of the bubble and slid along the ice.

Adora mounted Spirit. "I'll get your sceptre for you!" she cried.

"Better still," said Frosta, "take me with you."

She jumped up behind Adora, and Spirit galloped across the frozen lake to where the sceptre lay, still glowing with mystic light.

Frosta jumped down and picked it up.

"Let us out! Let us out!" cried Catra and Clawdeen.

"I will — but not yet!" said Frosta. "Not until I think that you have learned your lesson. You did your utmost to spoil the carnival. You disappointed all those who had worked hard building snowmen for the competition. Now, it is my turn to do something. I'm not going to build a snowman; I shall use my powers to make something special. Something that will be remembered as long as the carnival. And *you* will be part of it!"

Frosta raised the magic sceptre above her head.

From the Ice Empress's magic sceptre a stream of glittering ice crystals whirled through the air. Some were small as saucers. Others were big as cart-wheels. They spun and spiralled in the air. Then, as Frosta's magic power flowed from the sceptre, they began to gather around the shimmering blue bubble where Catra and Clawdeen were trapped.

The crystals clung to the bubble. Soon there was

nothing to be seen but the ice as it formed peaks and
pinnacles, domes and buttresses.

But wasn't there something familiar about it?

With a last flourish of her sceptre, Frosta sent a
sparkling stream of crystals which formed themselves
into a banner fluttering from an ice flagpole.

Almost at once, everyone cried: "THE CRYSTAL
CASTLE! Frosta has made the Crystal Castle out of
ice!"

With Catra and Clawdeen safely out of the way, everyone went back to enjoying their winter carnival.

Inside their icy prison, Catra and Clawdeen clung, shivering, together. From the edge of the lake the sounds of merriment reached them. And the breeze carried the smell of cooking.

"This is the last time I listen to your crazy ideas," said Clawdeen through chattering teeth. "Why can't you learn to leave well alone?"

There was a sound close by. Madame Razz had felt sorry for Catra and Clawdeen all alone out on the ice. Now, she came with some of the Twiggets. They all carried dishes of hot food. They managed to push it through odd cracks in the ice to the prisoners. Clawdeen growled, "Thank you," but Catra just sulked as she ate.

As the carnival came to an end, Frosta waved her sceptre, and the ice prison vanished. Catra and Clawdeen were free.

As they plodded back through the snow to Catra's tower, Clawdeen said, "At least, one of your dreams came true. You got your own Crystal Castle!"

Catra said nothing. She was too cold to think of anything to say.